Black Beauty

Written by Anna Sewell

Retold by Sue Purkiss

Illustrated by Kathryn Baker

Collins

Chapter 1

I stood under the trees by the pond beside my mother, getting my breath back. The sun was shining, the birds were singing and we'd just had the most marvellous gallop. I nuzzled her neck happily, and she whinnied in reply.

Just then, I noticed our master, Farmer Grey, entering the field with a man I hadn't seen before.

"Oh," said my mother. "That's Squire Gordon. I wonder … "

She sounded worried, but before I could ask what was wrong, the two men were in front of us.

"Here he is," said Farmer Grey proudly. "Isn't he a beauty? His grandfather won the races at Newmarket, you know. Twice!"

The squire looked at me thoughtfully. "Yes, he's certainly a fine horse. Not broken in, you say?"

The master shook his head. "No. Horses are like humans – they need their childhood, they need to play. But he's four now: he's ready. I'll see to the breaking in before he comes to you – if you're interested, that is?"

The squire looked at my eyes and into my mouth, and ran his hands up and down my legs. Then I had to walk, trot and gallop. After all that, he smiled. "Oh yes," he said. "I'm interested!"

As they walked away, my head was whirling with questions. I was to go away? I was to leave my mother? And I was to be *broken in*? What did it all mean?

My mother began to explain. "The job of a horse is to work for humans. We must carry them on our backs, we must pull their carriages, we must follow the hounds and hunt – we must do whatever we're told."

I soon learnt what this meant. We have to wear a harness. They put a bit in our mouths – a bar of cold, hard metal. Attached to this is a rein. When our rider or driver wants to give us an order, they pull on the rein, and then we know if they want us to turn, or to stop.

They have other, more painful ways of telling us what to do as well. They have whips. They have spurs, which bad riders dig into our sides till they draw blood.

I learnt that once a horse is broken in, he or she's no longer free. He can't roll in the grass when he feels like it. He can't have a good gallop whenever he wants to. He must just do as he's told – and hope he'll always have good masters who treat him well.

Being broken in after four years of freedom was hard to take, even with a good, kind master like Farmer Grey.

But leaving my mother was the worst thing. As I left our field to be taken to Squire Gordon's estate, I desperately wanted to break away and run back to her. But she'd taught me that I must always behave, always do as I was told. I turned my head to look at her one last time, and I thought my heart would break with sadness. I couldn't bear to think I might never see her again.

But that's how it is for horses.

Chapter 2

When I reached my new home, I was shown into
a light, roomy stable. In the next stall was Merrylegs,
a little grey pony who belonged to the squire's two
daughters, Flora and Jessie. He was very friendly
and liked to gossip, and he told me all about
the people at Birtwick Hall.

"The squire's a very good master," he told me.
"He won't put up with cruelty to horses – he'll tell
anyone off if he sees them treating an animal badly.
And the mistress – well, just wait till you meet her.
She's lovely. Then there's the coachman, John Manly.
He's very good too. He takes excellent care of us – wait
till you taste one of his bran mashes! Yes, we're very
lucky here."

I was beginning to feel much happier. But just then, a chestnut mare, Ginger, looked out from the stall beyond Merrylegs.

"Well, I don't think much to it," she said sniffily. "That was *my* stall, and I don't see why I had to be turned out for a young colt like you."

I started to apologise, even though it wasn't
my fault. But she just tossed her head and turned away.

"Don't worry about her," whispered Merrylegs.
"The truth is she snapped at Flora and Jessie. She's very
bad tempered. She hasn't been here long. John thinks
she'll get better, but I don't know … "

But John turned out to be right. Much later, when we'd become friends, Ginger told me she'd had a bad start. She'd been cruelly treated in her last two places – whipped till she bled, cut by spurs, and beaten when she didn't instantly do as she was told. So it really wasn't surprising that she'd started to lash out. At Birtwick, though, everyone was gentle with her, and she soon settled down and became much happier.

I felt very sorry for her. I'd had such a good start in life, and she'd had such a bad one. So I always looked out for her when we were in harness together, and calmed her down if anything startled her.

The first time the mistress came to see me, I took to her straight away. She had a soft voice and gentle hands, and she knew just where to stroke me – on the side of my neck, but also in that soft place between my eyes.

"Oh, he's beautiful!" she said. "Look at his glossy coat – and I love that white star on his forehead! I'm sure we're going to be great friends."

"He needs a new name," said the squire. "What do you think? What should we call him?"

She studied me. "Well, he's mostly black. And as I said, he's very beautiful. How about Black Beauty?"

And so that became my new name.

Sometimes the squire rode me, sometimes John did, and often I pulled one of the carriages, either with Ginger or by myself. But the best times were always when I carried the mistress. She had the lightest hand – she'd only to touch the rein and I knew just what she wanted me to do.

So when she fell ill, I missed her very much.
Then one night, I woke with a start – someone was
ringing the stable bell. What a noise! Soon after,
John came running in.

"Come on, Beauty," he said. "The mistress is
very bad and we must fetch the doctor. There's not
a moment to lose – if we don't hurry, it'll be too late!"

Well, I think my grandfather, the racehorse, would've been proud of me. I galloped as fast as I possibly could. When we got to the doctor's, John leapt off my back and hammered on the door.

As John spoke, the doctor ran his hand through his hair, looking worried.

"Of course I'll come, John," he said, "but I haven't got a horse. My son's taken one out on a call, and the other's laid up with a bad sprain. What to do? Can I take Beauty?"

John looked torn. "I've ridden him hard to get here – by rights he should rest. Well – needs must! But please be careful with him, sir – he's a good horse and I'd hate to have him hurt."

The doctor was heavier than John and not such a good rider. I had to use every ounce of my strength and I felt as if my heart was bursting. But I knew the mistress needed me and that drove me on.

At last, we reached the hall. The doctor dismounted and ran into the house to see to the mistress.

I stood there, exhausted, my sides heaving. John would've given me a rub down, a warm bran-mash and some warm water and covered me with a warm blanket.

But John wasn't there – he was still walking back from the doctor's. It was up to Joe Green, the new stable boy, who'd only been with us a few weeks. He did his best. He gave me cold water and corn, and didn't put a blanket on me because he thought I was already too hot.

By the time John got back, I was shivering and aching and I had a fever. It wasn't Joe's fault it was all wrong; he just didn't know any better, but it nearly killed me – I was ill for weeks. But Joe had learnt his lesson, and he became a very good stable boy.

Although that crisis was over, and John said I'd saved the mistress's life, she still didn't get better. In the end, the doctor said there was no help for it – she must go and live abroad where it was warmer. The house would be shut down, and we horses must all be sold.

I felt very sad. I would miss the master and mistress, and John Manly and little Joe. I would miss Merrylegs too.

But Ginger and I'd been sold to the same gentleman. I was thankful for that at least.

Chapter 3

Merrylegs went to the vicarage, where he already knew the people and they were fond of him.

Ginger and I were to go to a very grand estate called Earlshall, some 30 kilometres away. The earl was a friend of Squire Gordon, and I heard John say he'd promised to take good care of us.

I was anxious about the change, but at first all seemed well. The coachman, Mr York, who was in charge of the stables, all the grooms and the horses, knew his job. But he was no John Manly, and her ladyship was certainly no Mrs Gordon.

When she first saw us, she looked at us coldly.

"What's the meaning of this, York?" she said.
"You know their heads must be held high. They look
ridiculous. Why haven't you put on the bearing rein?"

Beside me, Ginger gave a low whinny of distress.

"They haven't been used to it, your ladyship. The
earl promised that they wouldn't have to wear it."

"Tosh! I won't have it – see to it immediately."

"But ... "

"Do it!"

Mr York sighed, and told one of the grooms to fetch the bearing rein.

Ginger had told me before about the bearing rein. She hated it. It was designed to force your head unnaturally high and keep it there. *It hurts your throat terribly*, she'd said. *And it makes it so hard when you go uphill – you can't put your head down and pull.*

"I won't put up with it," she whispered now. "I won't!"

To start with, it wasn't too bad.
But they fixed it tighter and
tighter, and one day, Ginger
had had enough. She reared
and lashed out with her
hooves, and it was sheer
luck that no one was
badly hurt.

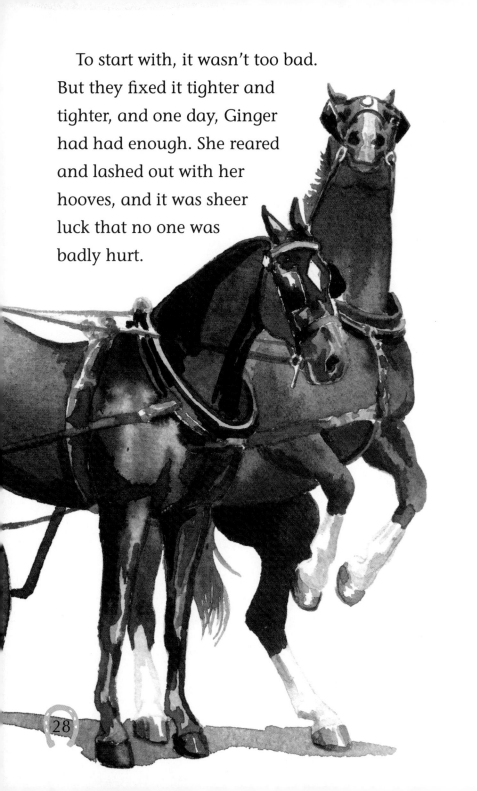

After that, she was given to one of the sons, Lord George, to use as a hunter. She preferred it, but he was a hard rider and she soon looked exhausted. Meanwhile, I had to put up with that cruel bearing rein for another four months, till at last the earl and her ladyship went up to London and I had a rest from it.

But worse was to come. Mr York had also gone to London, and the groom who was left in charge was called Reuben Smith. He was a lazy fellow, and without Mr York watching over him, things began to slide. One day, we had to take the carriage into town and leave it for some repairs. Before we set off for home, he quickly checked me over, and noticed there was a nail loose in one of my shoes. He frowned, and I heard him muttering to himself.

"Bother! If I take him to the blacksmith's to get his shoe fixed, I'll miss my supper ... Oh, it'll be all right till we get home!"

So off we went, with Reuben lashing me with
the whip, even though I was already going at a gallop.
Soon, of course, the nail worked loose and the shoe
came off. My hoof was cut and split on the sharp
stones – oh, how it hurt! But Reuben didn't notice
– he just kept using that cruel whip. I did my best,
but before long I stumbled and crashed onto
my knees, throwing Reuben to the ground.

Reuben lost his job, but that was no help to me. My knees were badly scarred, and though the earl was sorry for it, he said he couldn't have a damaged horse in his stable.

Ginger was in a bad way too. Lord George had strained her back and her windpipe by riding her too hard.

So, through no fault of our own, we were to be sold again.

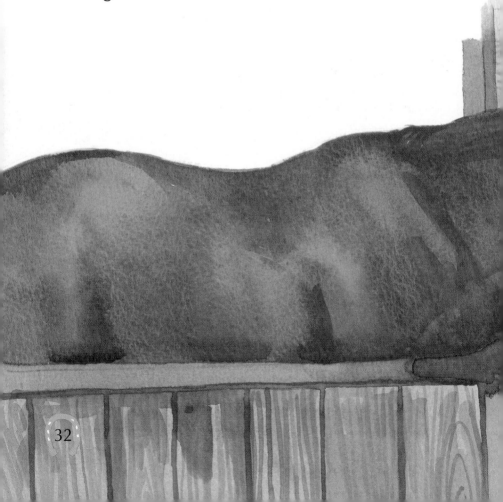

"Oh, Beauty," said Ginger sadly. "What's to become of us? Who'll want us now?"

I wished I could say something to cheer her up, but I knew she was right. We wouldn't be going to a better place – and this time, we wouldn't even be together. I touched her cheek with my muzzle, and we stood together in silence.

Chapter 4

I left first. Mr York knew of a livery stable in Bath, where – he said – I'd be well looked after. I neighed to Ginger as I was taken away, and she ran along the other side of the hedge as long as she could, calling to me anxiously. I didn't know what to expect, and I felt very nervous.

A livery stable is a place where horses and carriages are hired out to people who don't have a horse of their own. Sometimes they know how to handle a horse – but often they don't. They hold the reins too tight or too loose; they don't notice when a horse gets a stone in its shoe; they drive in the middle of the road so that they crash into a carriage coming the other way; they overload the carriage ... the real problem is that they don't consider the horse at all. It's just a means to an end – not a living creature with feelings and needs.

My mother always taught me to do my best, so I did – but it was very hard work.

Then, one day, a gentleman hired me who really knew how to drive. His hands were light on the rein, and he only touched me with the whip to show me what he wanted to do. He took a great liking to me, and he persuaded my master to sell me to a friend of his who wanted a good, safe horse to ride.

And so I went to Mr Barry.

He wanted a horse because his doctor had told him he needed exercise. But he knew nothing about horses or how to look after them. His first groom stole the oats I should've been given and sold them. I was soon out of condition and weak. A farmer friend spotted something was wrong; the thief was sacked and a new groom taken on. But he'd no more idea how to look after me than Mr Barry, and soon I was ill again.

By then, Mr Barry had had enough. I was on the move again.

Chapter 5

This time, I was taken to a horse fair to be sold.
It was a lively place, with all kinds of horses:
huge carthorses, little Welsh ponies, and many like
myself – good horses that had fallen on hard times.
But at the back I couldn't help but notice some very
poor-looking creatures. Their heads hung down,
their ribs stuck out and they looked utterly miserable.
I felt so sorry for them – and I felt afraid. What if I
ended up like that?

But now I had a stroke of luck. A man with a friendly smile and twinkling eyes came up and looked me over, talking to me softly. He made an offer and soon the deal was done. His name was Jerry Barker, and he was a cab driver from London. When we got home, I found his family were as nice as he was. His wife was Polly, his son, who was 12, was Harry, and his daughter, Dolly, was eight.

At last, I had a good home again. I had to work hard, picking up passengers and taking them wherever they wanted to go, but it was only for six days a week; on Sundays we had chance to rest and recover. He never drove me too fast or too far, and he always made sure I didn't have too much to carry. At first, I was frightened of the noise and bustle of the streets of London, but I got used to it before long. I soon grew fond of Jerry, and of Polly and the children, and I began to feel like part of the family.

One day, Jerry and I were waiting outside one of the parks when a cab drew up beside us. The horse was an old, worn-out chestnut – but there was something familiar about her. Suddenly I gasped. It was my dear old friend, Ginger!

But she looked terrible. She'd been such a beautiful horse, but now her joints were swollen, her coat was rough and she'd a terrible cough.

"Ginger," I whispered. "Is it really you?"

She lifted her head and stared at me. Then her dull eyes brightened. "Beauty!" she said. "I never thought I'd see you again! How wonderful – and you look so well!"

"But – what about you?" I said gently.

She shook her head wearily. "I'm as you see. This man's working me into the ground. I'm worn out, and I've no strength left. I can't bear it much longer. Honestly, Beauty, I wish I was dead!"

I touched my nose gently with hers, and I wished so much that I could do something to help her – it was awful seeing her like that.

She got her wish. Not long after, I saw a cart with a dead horse slung across it – a chestnut horse. It was Ginger. I could hardly bear it. She'd had such a sad, hard life, except for those three years at Squire Gordon's. At that moment, life seemed very cruel and miserable, and I realised how lucky I was to have an owner like Jerry.

Chapter 6

Like Ginger, Jerry was sometimes troubled with a
bad chest. One New Year's Eve, he had to fetch two
gentlemen from a card party at 11 o'clock. We arrived
there on time and settled down to wait. The weather had
turned very cold, and the rain turned to bitter, driving
sleet. At half past 12, Jerry rang the bell. They weren't
quite ready yet, he was told; he must wait a little longer.

By the time they came out, it was quarter
past one. Both Jerry and I were frozen, and he was
coughing badly. When we got home, he saw to me,
and then he disappeared inside.

For the next few days, it was Harry and Dolly
who looked after me – Jerry was dangerously ill
with bronchitis.

Both the children were quiet and worried. I never
saw Polly, because she hardly left his side.

Then, one day, I heard Dolly singing as she came into the stable.

"Oh, Beauty!" she said, flinging her arms round my neck. "Father's going to be all right! The doctor says he's turned the corner – isn't it wonderful?"

It was. But the doctor said that for the sake of his health, Jerry must give up cab driving. Being out in all weathers would kill him; that was all there was to it.

Luckily for the family, Jerry quickly found a job as a coachman to a lady called Mrs Fowler, who lived in the country. Polly had once worked for her, and she'd always said there'd be a job waiting for Jerry if he ever decided to give up cab driving. There was to be a cottage with a garden, apple trees and hens. They were all very excited.

And I was pleased for them. But what about me? Well, it was the usual story. I was to be sold. Where would I end up this time? I felt very troubled, and I feared the worst.

Chapter 7

The worst happened. I was bought by Nicholas
Skinner. He was a cab owner like Jerry, but the two
men were very different. My stable was cramped
and dark, so when I went out, the light was too bright
and I often stumbled. I was never allowed to rest, so I
just got more and more exhausted. I had to go long
distances, carrying too many passengers and too
much luggage. I was whipped till I bled, and I was
so miserable that, like Ginger, I began to think I'd be
better off dead.

One day, a huge pile of baggage was loaded on top of the cab. The daughter of the customer was distressed.

"Oh, Papa!" she said. "I'm sure this poor horse can't manage. He looks very weak."

But her father wouldn't listen. I did my best, as always, but this time it was just too much. I couldn't carry on. My feet slipped from under me, and I collapsed.

Skinner was all for shooting me – I heard him say it – but the vet persuaded him to let me rest and feed up for a couple of weeks.

"Then you'll be able to sell him. You'll get more for him that way," he urged.

Skinner thought about it and agreed. And that, thank goodness, was the last I saw of *him*. The vet looked after me till I was ready to be sold – and then it was off to the horse fair again.

"Look, Grandfather! What about this one? He's got a lovely mane and tail."

The old man looked me up and down. "Well – he has breeding, I'll say that for him."

"Oh, please! We can take him back to the farm and you can make him better, just like you did Ladybird. I'll do all the work. Please, Grandfather – please!"

He looked like a kind man, and I held my breath, hardly daring to hope.

He smiled, and put his arm round his grandson's shoulders. "All right then. Let's see what we can do for him."

The two of them cared for me all through the winter, and by March, I felt almost back to my old self. Three ladies were looking for a well-behaved carriage horse, and they decided I might suit.

There was something familiar about their groom. I stared at him, and he stared back. "Black all over," he muttered, "save for a white star and one white foot. And this little scar on your back ... I don't believe it! It's you, isn't it? It's Black Beauty! Why, it's a miracle!"

It was little Joe Green! I could hardly take it in. My heart felt very full as he flung his arms round my neck, and I remembered those happy days at Squire Gordon's.

So my story has ended well. If only Ginger's
had, too. But I'll never forget her, just as I'll never
forget any of the good people and horses I've met in
my long life. And tonight, when I've taken the ladies
out in their carriage and I'm home again, little Joe
Green will rub me down and give me a good feed,
then he'll turn me out into the field. Perhaps I'll stand
under the trees and dream of my
childhood, and that other field,
the one I shared all those
years ago with my
dear mother.

The fortunes and misfortunes of Black Beauty

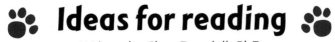

Ideas for reading

Written by Clare Dowdall, PhD
Lecturer and Primary Literacy Consultant

Reading objectives:
- identify and discuss themes and conventions in and across a wide range of writing
- check that the book makes sense to them, discuss their understanding and explore the meaning of words in context
- draw inferences such as inferring characters' feelings, thoughts and motives from their actions, and justifying inferences with evidence
- predict what might happen from details stated and implied

Spoken language objectives:
- participate in discussions, presentations, performances, role play, improvisations and debates

Curriculum links: PSHE – relationships

Resources: ICT for research; pens and paper

Build a context for reading

- Look at the front cover and ask children to share what they know about the story of Black Beauty.
- Talk about children's experiences of horses. Discuss the special relationship that some people have with horses, and build a word bank to describe this.
- Ask children to read the blurb. Based on this, ask them to predict what kinds of events might happen in this story.

Understand and apply reading strategies

- Read Chapter 1 to the children. Discuss who is speaking and what can be inferred about the narrator.
- Ask children to look for evidence that the story is set in the past. Encourage them to share their ideas, referring to the story and language used ("squire", "master").
- Discuss what the phrase "breaking in" means, and how it would feel to be in Beauty's position when he learns from his mother that his life is to change forever.